THIS BOOK
BELONGS TO:

mantra lingua

_____

_____

_____

For Anna
M.W.

For Sebastian,
David & Candlewick
H.O.

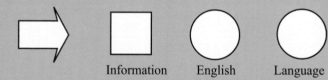

Information   English   Language

Published by arrangement with Walker Books Ltd, London SE11 5HJ

Dual language edition first published 2006 by Mantra Lingua
Dual language TalkingPEN edition first published 2010 by Mantra Lingua
Global House, 303 Ballards Lane, London N12 8NP, UK
http://www.mantralingua.com

Text copyright © 1991 Martin Waddell
Illustrations copyright © 1991 Helen Oxenbury
Dual language text and audio copyright © 2006 Mantra Lingua
This edition edition 2011

A CIP record of this book is available from the British Library

Printed in Malta GC080611PB0711

L'anatra contadina
FARMER DUCK

written by
MARTIN WADDELL

illustrated by
HELEN OXENBURY

MANTRA LINGUA

C'era una volta un'anatra che aveva la sfortuna
di vivere con un vecchio contadino pigro.
L'anatra faceva tutto il lavoro.
Il contadino stava a letto tutto il giorno.

There once was a duck who had the bad luck
to live with a lazy old farmer.
The duck did the work.
The farmer stayed
all day in bed.

L'anatra andava a prendere la mucca al pascolo.
"Come va il lavoro?" gridava il contadino.
L'anatra rispondeva:
"Qua qua!"

The duck fetched the cow from the field.
"How goes the work?"
called the farmer.
The duck answered,
"Quack!"

L'anatra riportava le pecore dalla collina.
"Come va il lavoro?" gridava il contadino.
L'anatra rispondeva:
"Qua qua!"

The duck brought the sheep from the hill.
"How goes the work?" called the farmer.
The duck answered,
"Quack!"

L'anatra metteva le galline nel pollaio.
"Come va il lavoro?" gridava il contadino.
L'anatra rispondeva:
"Qua qua!"

The duck put the hens in their house.
"How goes the work?"
called the farmer.
The duck answered,
"Quack!"

Il contadino s'ingrassava a furia di stare a letto e
la povera anatra era stufa di lavorare tutto il giorno.

The farmer got fat through staying in bed
and the poor duck got fed up
with working all day.

"Come va il lavoro?"
"QUA QUA!"

"How goes the work?"
"QUACK!"

"Come va il lavoro?"
"QUA QUA!"

"How goes the work?"
"QUACK!"

"Come va il lavoro?"
"QUA QUA!"

"How goes the work?"
"QUACK!"

"Come va il lavoro?"
"QUA QUA!"

"How goes the work?"
"QUACK!"

La povera anatra aveva sonno e
voglia di piangere ed era stanca.

The poor duck was sleepy
and weepy
and tired.

Le galline e la mucca e le pecore erano
molto preoccupate.
Volevano bene all'anatra. Allora fecero
una riunione al chiarore della luna e
prepararono un piano per la mattina.

"MUU!" disse la mucca.
"BEE!" dissero le pecore.
"COCCODÈ!" dissero le galline.
E QUELLO era il piano!

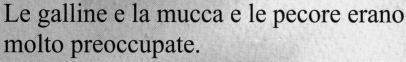

The hens and the cow
and the sheep got very
upset.
They loved the duck.
So they held a meeting
under the moon and
they made a plan
for the morning.

"MOO!" said the cow.
"BAA!" said the sheep.
"CLUCK!" said the hens.
And THAT was the plan!

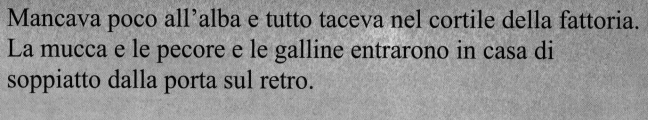

Mancava poco all'alba e tutto taceva nel cortile della fattoria.
La mucca e le pecore e le galline entrarono in casa di
soppiatto dalla porta sul retro.

It was just before dawn and the farmyard was still.
Through the back door and into the house
crept the cow and the sheep and the hens.

Attraversarono furtivamente l'ingresso. Salirono per le scale scricchiolanti.

They stole down the hall.
They creaked
up the stairs.

Si strinsero sotto il letto del contadino e si dimenarono. Il letto iniziò a ondeggiare e il contadino si svegliò e gridò: "Come va il lavoro?" e...

They squeezed under the bed of the farmer and wriggled about. The bed started to rock and the farmer woke up, and he called, "How goes the work?" and...

"MUU!"
"BEE!"
"COCCODÈ!"

"MOO!"
"BAA!"
"CLUCK!"

Gli animali sollevarono il letto e il vecchio
contadino cominciò a strillare. A furia di colpi
lo sbatterono di qua e di là, e di là e di qua,
fino a buttarlo fuori dal letto...

They lifted his bed and he started to shout, and they banged
and they bounced the old farmer about and about and about,
right out of the bed...

e lui scappò, con la mucca e le pecore e le galline
che muggivano e belavano e chiocciavano attorno a lui.

and he fled with the cow and the sheep and the hens
mooing and baaing and clucking around him.

Lungo il sentiero...
"Muu!"

Down the lane...
"Moo!"

per i campi...
"Bee!"

through the fields...
"Baa!"

su per la collina...
"Coccodè!"

over the hill...
"Cluck!"

e non tornò mai più.

and he never came back.

L'anatra si svegliò e si trascinò
dondolando stancamente nel
cortile, aspettandosi di sentire:
"Come va il lavoro?"
Ma nessuno parlò!

The duck awoke and waddled wearily into the yard expecting
to hear, "How goes the work?"
But nobody spoke!

Poco dopo tornarono la mucca e le pecore e le galline.

"Qua qua?" chiese l'anatra.

"Muu!" disse la mucca.

"Bee!" dissero le pecore.

"Coccodè!" dissero le galline.

E in questo modo raccontarono tutta la storia all'anatra.

Then the cow and the sheep and the hens came back.

"Quack?" asked the duck.

"Moo!" said the cow.

"Baa!" said the sheep.

"Cluck!" said the hens.

Which told the duck
the whole story.

Poi, muggendo e belando e chiocciando e
facendo qua qua, si misero tutti a lavorare
nella loro fattoria.

Then mooing and baaing
and clucking and quacking
they all set to work
on their farm.

小李的农历新年
Li's Chinese New Year

દીપકની દિવાળી
Deepak's Diwali
Divya Karwal
Doreen Long

Wigilia z Markiem i Alicją
Marek and Alice's Christmas

L'Eid de Samira
Samira's Eid

Digirinkii Dhali Jirtay
Beedka Dahabka ah
The Goose that Laid
the Golden Egg ...
Shaun Chauo
Jago

Àwon Àhuso
Ìtàn Kòlòkòlò
Fox Fables
Dawn Casey
Jago

La Liebre y la Tortuga
the HARE and the TORTOISE

Басни о льве
LION FABLES
by JAN ORMEROD
RUSSIAN AND ENGLISH

Here are some other bestselling

dual language books from Mantra Lingua

for you to enjoy.

三隻山羊加菲
The Three
Billy Goats Gruff
Henriette Barkow
Illustrated by Richard Johnson

Ricitos de Oro y los tres ositos
Goldilocks and the Three Bears
Kate Clynes
Louise Daykin

ADÌE PUPA KÉKERÉ ÀTI
ÈSO ÀLÌKÁMÀ
The Little Red Hen and the
Grains of Wheat
L. R. Hen
Jagó

The Buskers of Bremen
by Henriette Barkow Illustrated by Nathan Reed

Неужели опять,
Красная Шапочка!
Not Again, Red Riding Hood!
Kate Clynes & Louise Daykin

Füchslein Sly und
Hühnchen Little Red!
Sly Fox and Little Red Hen!
Henriette Barkow
Richard Johnson

跟上齊達
Lindsay Camp
Jill Newton
Keeping Up With Cheetah

Ecoute, Ecoute
Listen, Listen
Phillis Gershator,
Alison Jay